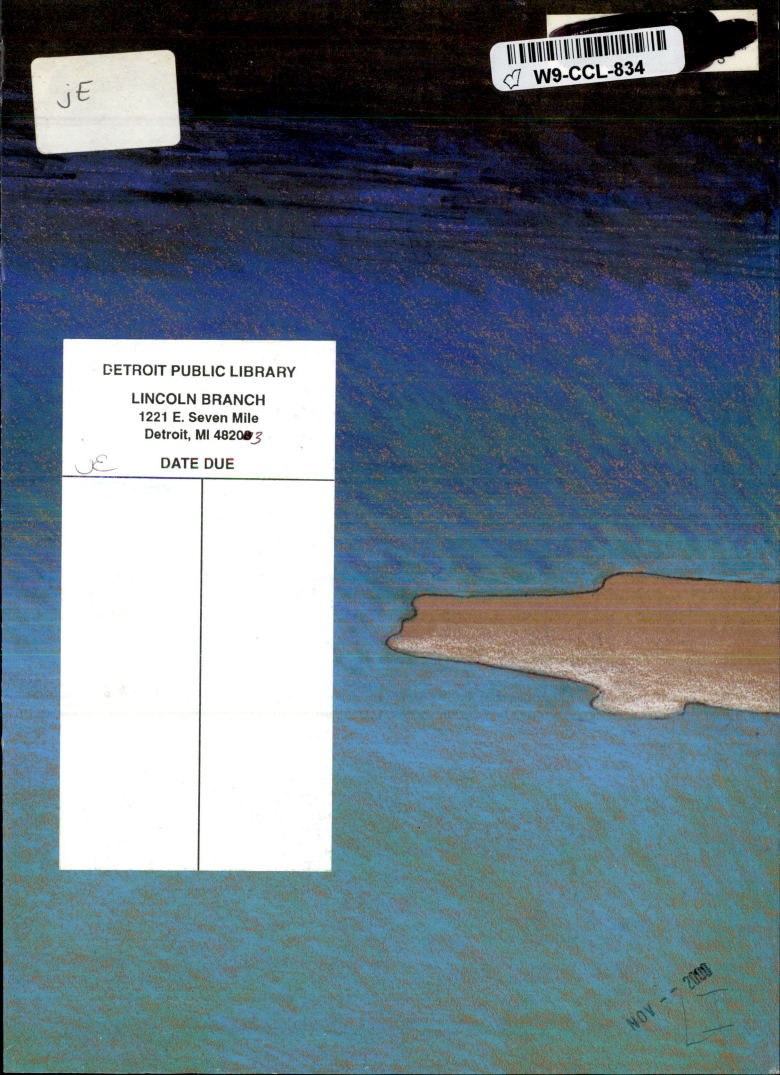

jE

W9-CCL-834

DETROIT PUBLIC LIBRARY

LINCOLN BRANCH
1221 E. Seven Mile
Detroit, MI 48203

DATE DUE

NOV -- 2000

Harriet Ziefert and Seymour Chwast

MOONRIDE

HOUGHTON MIFFLIN COMPANY BOSTON 2000

Walter Lorraine Books

This one is for James.
HZ

This one is for Miss P., Miss M. and Mr. M.
SC

Walter Lorraine (wл) Books

Text copyright © 2000 by Harriet Ziefert
Illustrations copyright © 2000 by Seymour Chwast

All rights reserved. For information about permission to
reproduce selections from this book, write to
Permissions, Houghton Mifflin Company, 215 Park Avenue South,
New York, New York 10003.

Library of Congress Cataloging-in-Publication Data

Ziefert, Harriet.
       Moonride by Harriet Ziefert: Illustrated by Seymour Chwast.
       p. cm.
       Summary: Presents a guide to proper behavior for the
child fortunate to catch a ride through the night with the moon.
       ISBN 0-618-00229-4
       [1. Moon—Fiction. 2. Night—Fiction.] I. Chwast, Seymour, ill. II. Title.
PZ7.C487Mk 2000
[E]—dc21   99-13458
                                                  CIP

Printed in China for Harriet Ziefert, Inc.
HZI 10 9 8 7 6 5 4 3 2 1

NOV - - 2000
L1

If the moon wakes you up in the middle
of the night and offers you a ride,

say yes.

But make sure he promises to have you
back in your bed before the sun comes up.

When you're in the air, hang on tight.

Don't ask too many questions about where
you're going and when you'll get there.

When the moon finds you a seat right behind home plate, politely thank him.

And when at the top of the eighth inning he says it's time to go, don't complain.

If there's smoke, don't be frightened.

When the moon stops at a bakery for a snack,
thank the baker for the warm blueberry muffin.

Put it in your pocket. You might get hungry later.

While the moon is waiting for a cup of coffee,
you may want to use the bathroom.

While the moon reads the morning paper,
be patient. Don't interrupt.

It should take him only a few minutes to glance at
the front-page headlines and the weather forecast.

Don't look down!

Relax and enjoy the jazzy music.

If it looks like you may be headed straight for a bridge,

don't panic. Stay calm.

Someone will dial 911-WIND to ask for help.

You're safe! Get comfortable again.

Don't ask "Are we there yet?"

or "How much longer until I'm home?"

Remain seated until the moon has come to a complete stop.
Remember to take all of your belongings with you.

Thank the moon for an interesting evening.

And when your mother asks if you've had sweet dreams,

say YES!